Kissing

Snakes

PRELUDE TO SERIES

UNBELIEVABLE ADVENTURES OF ERIK JANSEN

Jack Tenor

This book is a work of fiction. Names, characters, places and incidents are products of the author's imagination or are used fictitiously. Any resemblance to events or locales or persons, living or dead, is entirely coincidental.

Copyright © 2024 Jack Tenor

All rights reserved. No part of this publication may be reproduced, stored in a retrieval system, or transmitted, in any form, or by any means (electronic, mechanical, photocopying, recording or otherwise) without the prior written permission of the author.

ISBN: 9798325917875

I dedicate this book to all people in the world who fought against Nazis and their regime during the dark days of occupation. Thank you for all you did for us.

Jack Tenor

TABLE OF CONTENT

1	1
2	5
3	9
4	14
5	18
6	23
7	27
8	31
9	36
10	42
11	46
12	54
13	60
14	64
15	67
16	72

Chapter 1

I took a last sip and swished the Scotch around, keeping it in my mouth as long as I could stand the fire. The peaty sensation filled my throat. It was an excellent whiskey. Just as I liked it. No rocks.

The fat, bald barman stared at the photograph as if he had never seen a young girl in his life. Two more seconds, and I would snatch it back. The picture could fade out from his nasty glance. He scratched his beard and returned the photograph to the counter.

"I've never seen her," he said, shaking his head. "Who is she?"

"My aunt," I said, hiding the photograph in my jacket.

"Little young for your aunt, don't you reckon?"

"Grandma adopted her."

He shook his head again and grabbed the bottle. "One more?"

"No. Got things to do."

"Why are you looking for her?"

"She stole my money."

"Your aunt?"

"She's not my aunt."

"Why did you say she was?"

"I didn't."

He sighed. "I don't understand that humor of yours, Erik."

"You know what? No one does," I said and slipped off the bar stool. The last thing on my list was to spill the beans to a man who profited from pouring drinks for Nazis and serving them food.

The poorly lit bar was almost empty, as was my stomach, not counting the drink I'd just had. Two groups of Nazi soldiers in SS uniforms sat behind the tables, playing cards. Their sharp voices rattled the glasses on the shelf of the back bar. The soldiers argued. Spending the night here would mean broken chairs and lips.

"How did she steal your money, huh? A hooker, right?" He chuckled. "Your father would be ashamed if he was still among us. I knew him well. He was a great cop. Always stopped by to have a talk and a shot of Jenever. Those were better times than now."

This jerk dared to put my father's name to his filthy mouth. My father had died a year ago. No. He had been killed a year ago thanks to dirty rats like this one. I fought with the urge to spit into his face. I won. He wasn't worth it. Not now.

"Yeah, he introduced me to her."

I nodded toward the soldiers. "Having more and more Uncle Heini's fellas over, huh? This bar goes a Titanic's path."

"The times are cruel, Erik. I need to pay rent and feed a family."

His insincere voice betrayed him. Not that it mattered. Everyone knew he grew piglets on a small farm in a nearby village. He sold the meat on the black market for a pretty penny. That wouldn't be bad. Many did the same. But what he didn't sell, he made schnitzels and goulash, offering them to Nazi officers for lunch. Often for free, gaining privileges. My spine shivered. *Jeez, this used to be my favorite bar.*

"Thank God you're not an actor, Henk," I said, tossing him a coin. "That would be the worst movie I have ever watched."

He snapped the coin out of the air and hid it behind his stained apron.

"If you see her, let me know."

"I will. You can trust me."

You bet I will, moron.

Before I left, I obeyed nature's call and headed toward the toilets. Like almost anywhere else, the separated toilets shared a small doorway with a sink, a long mirror, and a small bin. I opened the door. The image I saw rocketed my blood pressure through the roof. Perhaps it was my grandpa's voice telling me not to hurt my younger sister when we fought. Or the environment I had grown up in. I didn't care. I couldn't stand a man hitting a woman.

"I'm sorry to disturb you, but I heard your friends calling you," I said in a voice loud enough to be heard in Paris.

The bloke wearing the SS uniform ignored my attempt to be polite and pulled his arm back. His other hand was gripping the girl's throat. Her red right cheek yelled she'd already met his dirty palm. Her lips twitched in a muted scream. I grasped his hand right when he swung it. The momentum turned him around. He was taller than me by a head and a half.

"I guess the lady clearly suggested she wanted to leave," I said.

He yanked his hand from my grip and released the girl's throat. His glittering eyes swam in alcohol, as did his breath. His hand pulled back again, aiming to hit me, but my leg sprung forward hard, and the bloke crouched in pain, pressing his palms against his crotch and clenching his teeth. I'd been good at soccer since I could remember. I smashed his head against the wall. The wall rumbled. Or was it his head? No one cared. I watched his consciousness taking off and leaving him stretched out on the floor.

"I'm sorry you had to see this, but I had no other option," I said to the girl and tried to pull the corners of my mouth into an apologizing grin.

She could be eighteen, maybe nineteen years old. Perhaps less. Dark shoulder-cut hair covered by a tiny top hat with a net over her face, all in harmony with her navy polka sailor dress. Deep maroon eyes wetted by the terror she went through. She held a small purse, pressing it against her chest.

"Don't worry," I said in a calming voice. "He won't hurt you."

I did my stuff and left the room. The girl was gone. The filthy pig lay on the floor. I checked his pulse and his head. No traces of blood. Good. Not that I would have regretted spilling his blood or felt sorry for him. No. Killing him could ruin my task, though.

I strolled out, passing the Nazis still playing cards and pouring schnapps into their mouths like it was water. They didn't miss their comrade. Perhaps they thought he was enjoying his little action. Or maybe not. I didn't give a shit.

Chapter 2

The street was calm. The sun had already found its way down, sending its last beams through the cloudless blue summer sky. The heavy-to-breathe air was still hot. I gazed at the line of buildings along the Shinkel channel, counting how many bars stood on this side of the street. This was going to be a long night.

My stomach growled. I had better grab some food before I continued the round trip. An empty tummy could cope with one whiskey. Perhaps two would do no harm. But three? A waste of money.

I had to find that girl. Dortje, Dirk Smit's daughter. The Dirk Smit who'd had to hide since the Nazis had seized his metalworking factory. He wanted to leave for Latin America, but not without her. So, the old man hired me. Someone could've kidnapped the seventeen-year-old girl to lure Mr. Smit from his hideout. There was a reward on his head. No, not money. The Nazis had found other benefits for their pets. Abandoned stores or small manufactories once run by people sent to camps.

Someone touched my shoulder. I was startled. It was her. The girl I'd helped out.

"Girl! For God's sake!" I said. "Do you want me to put something into my pants?"

"Are you Erik Jansen?" she said in a low voice.

"Who's asking?"

"Do you remember me? I am Suus Achter. I went to the same school as you."

Achter? An image of a little schoolgirl with two pigtails flashed through my mind. Not the face, though.

She must have read my thoughts. "I'm Bram Achter's sister. The barber. He was your schoolmate. Do you remember?"

I nodded. Who the hell was Bram Achter?

"You all called him Piggy."

Oh, crap! I had forgotten. Piggy, the bloke with the fantastic talent for mimicking oinking, hence the nickname.

I gazed at her. The Piggy's little sister was no longer little and less sister than my relation to the British king. I'd heard about her in the last couple of months. Her reputation was terrible. Piggy's little sister was a hooker. Not that I minded hookers. I didn't care. Rumors were told in the neighborhood that this young lady did things that passed beyond my, otherwise exceptionally open-minded acceptance, like lying with Nazis for money.

"And?" I said.

"I want to thank you for helping me."

"No need." I shook my head. "Next time, run away from those blokes. That would help you more than any hard fist in this city."

"I know what people say about me, and it's…"

"Next time, do as I tell you. Run away."

She sighed and played the flip side. "You are looking for Doortje Smit, aren't you?" she whispered.

I believed tomorrow's newspapers would write about it on the front page. Where the hell had she heard about it?

She stepped closer. "We were schoolmates like you and Bram. I was with her that last night. I was the last person who saw her. She argued with her father. About Latin America. Doortje didn't want to leave for Argentina. She wanted to go to New York to her aunt." Her eyes widened as if she had discovered a new planet, or an extinct animal hidden in a cave under the sea.

"That's a very compelling story. Really is. You should write a book. I want to read it."

"You don't believe me, do you?"

I would bet she had something to do with the kidnappers of the poor girl. None of the words she was saying made sense. Why would the daughter of a wealthy man have gone to the same lyceum as a girl from an ordinary Dutch family? Even fish in Amsterdam's channels talked about Doortje returning from the boarding school for young ladies in Paris before the occupation.

"Never mind." Suus checked to see if we were alone. "I'll tell you anyway. She ran away from her father. I met her at the Cafe Karpershoek. She told me everything. I needed to go to the toilet. A bald man was talking to her. When I returned, she was gone. In the morning, I visited her father, Mr. Smit. I was curious if she was all right. He told me you're looking for her. I came here to meet you, but that soldier…"

I waited for her to finish her sweet story. Tonight, I wasn't a buyer. Did she want me to tell her where Mr. Smit was hiding?

"You don't believe me, Erik."

I sighed. "I believe you. Thank you for letting me know. After all, there are only three or four bald men in Amsterdam, right? It would be easier for me if it were true. But I'm not looking for anyone. I'm looking for a tasty, cheap dinner and an opportunity to get drunk. Anyway, here's a tenner for you. For your effort." I handed her the bill.

Her eyes wet. Never trust a face that cries so much. "I'm telling the truth. I don't need your money."

"Everyone needs my money. The landlady, taxmen, doctors. You would be surprised, but even coffee is not free in this city."

"You know nothing, Erik. You judge me like anyone else does."

"Me? Lady, I don't care," I said and left her standing there, tucking the tenner back into my pocket.

Shit! Someone knew Dirk Smit wanted to leave Amsterdam. They must have drugged Doortje, and she'd spat out everything. A part of Suus's story was true. Mr. Smit had told me they argued and then she left. I should have a peek at Cafe Karpershoek. But not now. Now, my steps led somewhere else. Doortje could have talked about their hideout as well. Crucial to check on the old man. My stomach growled again. This would be a long night. My tummy would have to wait.

Chapter 3

The water boiled in the kettle. I moved it off the stove. The boiling stopped, and I spilled two teaspoons of ground coffee in and returned the kettle to the stove. The bubbles developed again. The sharp smell filled my small flat. I let the foam grow, moving the kettle off the stove right when it wanted to go over the kettle rim. That was the way of brewing coffee a friend from Bosnia had taught me. The right way.

Last night was a complete disaster. After swerving and stopping at a couple of bars, I'd arrived at the flat where Mr. Smit was hiding. I had knocked using the secret signal. No one opened. The lock on the door was an easy toy. Any child could have opened it with a piece of wire. The flat was empty. No traces of violence, though. Dirk Smit had left of his own accord, leaving no clues where he had gone.

Sitting on the worn-out chair behind the table, I sipped the hot drink and contemplated my next steps. The sun shone straight into my sleepy face. I closed my eyes and ignored the need to go back to bed.

I'd slept only for two hours because, after leaving Mr. Smit's hideout, I'd continued combing bars, showing the girl's photograph wherever I could. People just stared at it. The only words I got from them were about how pretty she was. Come on, people, I wasn't showing you the picture of my fiancée and expecting praise. The girl had evaporated into thin air just like that. I should find Suus again and ask inconvenient questions.

The coffee mug was empty. I stood up and paced toward the fridge to get some eggs and butter. I could only dream of fresh bread; the bakery down the street wasn't selling anymore. Its owner disappeared a week ago. I could only guess where. The kitchenette provided me with a satisfactory ability to make breakfast and, now and then, some light dinner. I lunched outdoors every day.

Someone banged on the door. A glimpse at the clock on the wall showed it was still early. Who the hell would disturb me at seven in the morning? I wasn't expecting any visitors. Could be the old lady from the neighboring flat had locked herself out again. I suspected she did that on purpose, seizing the opportunity to talk. A slight warm chitchat cheered her up. Her husband and son had died in the first war.

I opened the door. The prepared smile froze on my face. I gazed at the two coppers. That piece of crap I'd knocked down yesterday must have talked. Bloody coward.

"Erik Jansen?" said the one who stood closer to the door.

I nodded.

"You need to come with us."

"Come where?"

"To the police station."

"Why?"

"You'll see."

"I want to hear it now."

"I don't care what you want. Take your coat or whatever, and come before I break your legs."

"If you break my legs, you will have to carry me. You should break my hands. That would do better."

The second cop stepped closer. "Erik, don't make problems. The Senior Constable needs to ask you a couple of questions. That's all. You're not in trouble. You have my word.

I've known you since you were a child. I won't allow anyone to harm you."

"And that should help me how?"

He said nothing.

I didn't trust any policeman since my father's death. Especially not those who talked about him. Running away would've been the most stupid thing, though. My jacket hung next to the door. I took it, stepped out, and locked the door. They seated me in the back of the car. For a moment, I felt like a king with all the pomp. Or a victim for a ritual sacrifice. *Oh, shit!* I had forgotten to put the eggs back into the fridge. The day looked warm. I hoped I wouldn't find baby chickens on the kitchenette top when I returned.

Thinking about that scumbag Beekhof who wanted to ask me questions made me want to kill someone. He was the man who'd stabbed my father in the back when the Nazis took over the gendarmery in our district. Not word for word, though. The police then created two groups. One supported the change and gained plenty of privileges. The second group suffered. My father, who was the Senior Constable at that time, became unwanted, causing trouble and refusing to give up. They shot him during a bust in the docks. Beekhof had gotten his chair overnight.

We arrived, and the two coppers led me straight to Beekhof's office. The so-called friend knocked on the door and opened it. He disappeared inside, saying something I couldn't hear. The door opened wide, and I stepped in. Beekhof sat behind the desk. Behind my father's desk! I clenched my fists. He was eating breakfast, tucking a sausage into his greasy mouth.

"Sit down," he said, pointing his finger at the wooden chair in the middle of the room.

The chair complained when I sat on it, creaking like a cat after a long nap. How many souls had sat here, trying to escape jail? Who could tell?

"I haven't had my breakfast yet. May I take a piece of bread?" I said.

He swallowed, staring at me with a face that disgusted me more than anything.

"This will be quick. Then you can go home," he said.

He wiped his chin with a crumpled handkerchief and stood up. Taking a piece of paper from the desk, he handed it to me. I reached with both hands. It was a photograph of a young girl. I knew she was around seventeen years old. She lay on the ground, wearing a dark dress decorated with white dots. Her throat was cut, and her head swam in the dark pool. Despite the photograph being in shades of gray, I was sure it was blood. The young girl in the picture was dead. Her name was Suus Achter.

"Did you know her?" he said.

I nodded.

"When did you see her the last time?"

"Yesterday. We met at Jan's bar close to Schinkelhavenstraat bridge."

"How long did you know her?"

I told him the entire story, keeping the adventure with the SS soldier out. And, of course, Doortje Smit.

"What happened then?"

"Nothing. I went to another bar."

He nodded and returned to the desk. "I know that, Erik. I needed to hear it from you. People saw you. With her before Jan's bar and then alone in Ernest's bar, and later in two more bars."

"Where was she found?"

"Down at the channel bank right before the bar you met her in. She lay under the gangway. Do you want to tell me something more?"

"There's nothing more I know. She recognized me. I went to school with her brother. That's it."

He leaned forward. His eyebrows drew together.

"Do you have something to do with this?"
"No."
"Are you sure?"
"More sure about this than about my breakfast."
"Why did you visit so many bars?"
"I don't like to sit on one chair for the entire night."

He gazed at me, his cheeks puffed. His effort to look threatening was lame. He looked as if he was sitting on the toilet and fighting with constipation.

"I'll let you go, Erik. For the sake of friendship with your father."

My nails dug into the skin of my palms.

"But! If I figure out you lied to me, I will send you to the gallows. Do you understand?"

I nodded.

"Now, go!"

I left the police station and headed to a nearby diner. What had this been about? Beekhof wanted to show his power, and nothing was clearer than that. But why? I didn't find any logical reason. He was just a jerk who had no idea what he was doing. Someone had told him about me, and he'd used the opportunity to seize the son of his past adversary and shoot blind. Like, he hadn't asked me what we'd been talking about or where she'd gone after. I wouldn't have told him, anyway.

Suus' words echoed in my mind. The poor gal had been telling the truth. I had to find out who the bald man was that Doortje had been talking to.

Chapter 4

After breakfast, I headed to the barbershop where Bram Achter had cut hair and trimmed beards. I hadn't talked to him since we left the school, not counting small talk when we occasionally met on the street. From time to time, people spread rumors about him and his sister. Like about anyone else. Besides the barbershop, he sold stuff on the black market. I didn't know what, and I didn't care.

His small shop stood at the corner next to Vondelkerk, the church. Strolling there relaxed me. The streets around Vondelpark were not over-packed by patrols like around Euterpestraat or in Jordaan, the quarter overpopulated mostly by poor people.

The door had a cute little bell, held by a brass angel in one hand. Its sound was cute, too. Two vanity tables, comfortable chairs, and the scent of cologne. I liked it.

"Erik!" he said and jumped off the chair, spreading his arm like I was a wealthy uncle lost for a long time somewhere in Amazonia and packed with diamonds.

"Piggy!" I said. "Oh, I'm sorry, Bram. The habit, you know."

"No need to apologize. You called me that, then. And know you what? I was proud of it." He grinned.

"That's true. No one could ever grunt just like you did."

Bram oinked. It was loud and so real; I got hungry again. We laughed.

"What can I do for you, Erik?"

I scratched my cheek. "See my face? It desperately needs shaving. I guess you can do something with this."

"Sure, my friend. Take a seat. You are my first customer I can't remember since when."

I sat in the barber chair, watching myself in the large mirror. He prepared his stuff, wetted my face and neck, and started to soap the surface enriched by my facial hair. He talked a lot. Mostly about things I knew or things I didn't care about. Every so often, he stopped soaping and waved his hands, strengthening his words with gestures. The soap foam flew from the brush everywhere. I let him talk.

He took the razor and began to scrape the soap off my neck, pulling the blade upward. I waited for the moment when he cleaned it, wiping the foam over his thumb.

"Bram, I'm here because of your sister."

He put the razor on my neck, holding it there without moving and gazing at the reflection of my face in the mirror. I reached from under the large towel he put over my shoulders and chest and nudged his hand away.

"I'm sorry about what happened. It's a tragedy," I said.

He didn't move. His hand hung forgotten in the air, ready to cut through my throat.

"I'd like to ask you a few questions."

"Are you a copper? Like your father was?" he said.

"No, I'm not. A private detective, that's what I am. An eye working for a client, and..."

"Who's he?"

"That's confidential. The thing is, I talked with Suus yesterday."

"Do you know something?"

"No, I don't. The only thing I know is that my case is somehow connected with Suus' death."

"How?"

"I don't know yet. That's why I'm here."

Bram continued to shave in perfect strokes, keeping silent. I shut my mouth as well. He finished and wiped the remains of the soap with the small towel he'd taken from the pile on the side of the mirror. Then he splashed an aftershave on his hands and massaged it into my skin, patting over my cheeks.

"People didn't know her," he said, and a lone tear ran down his cheek. "Everyone gossiped like crazy without caring about the truth."

I said nothing.

Bram sat on the next chair and lit a cigarette.

"She was a hooker. That's true. But she never lay with Nazis. Never. That was a lie spread by envious neighbors. As if there was something to envy. And no one has ever cared why she did what she did. She could study at the university. She could be a doctor. That smart she was!"

More tears appeared, and he wiped them off his face with the same towel he forgot to put aside.

"No one cares that we have a seriously sick mother. Erik, my mom is dying, and no one knows why. We've tried everything, but it costs money we don't have. All that Suus earned, and all that I earned, went for medicaments that didn't help. Now, what I'm going to do? Money from this shop or from selling the salt in the market is not enough."

The silence that followed could be cut with his razor.

"I'm sorry to hear that, Bram," I said in a low voice. "I'd like to help you, but I don't know how. But, perhaps I can find who killed Suus. She mentioned a bald man. Does it ring any bells?"

He shook his head.

"Think, Bram. Any small details can help."

"She never said anything about a bald man. She didn't like to talk about… her job."

"Perhaps it wasn't connected to her job."

"No. Nothing. No bells."

I took a photograph with Doortje's picture and showed it to him.

"Have you met this girl?"

"Sure, that's Doortje Smit. They were best friends during primary school. Doortje then left for Paris. What it has to do with…"

"Nothing. Forget it." I put the photograph back in my pocket. A lump developed in my throat. Hard to swallow. My lips whispered apologies to Suus. I'd been stupid.

"There's one thing, though," he said.

"What?"

"She walked the streets often with Lena, a German girl."

"Where can I find her?"

"Oh, you don't know? What a detective!" He grinned. It felt good to see him smile a bit. "They worked at the Cafe Karpershoek."

I stood up and handed him a tenner.

"That's too big. I don't have change."

"Keep it."

"No, Erik. That's too much."

I put the bill on the table. "Keep it. I'm not doing it for you or for your mother. I'm doing it for me. By taking the money, you'll provide me with a service. It's my redemption."

"Redemption?"

"Don't think about it too long, please."

We said goodbye, and I left his shop. An enormous cloud hid the sun, and I felt sick. I couldn't have saved the poor gal even if I'd believed her instead of judging her. Remorse wouldn't help, though. I had to find the bald man. The bloke appeared to be more and more interesting. *Let's have a rendezvous with Lena, whoever she is.*

Chapter 5

Groups of Nazi officers strolled around the Cafe Karpershoek, heading for lunch in small restaurants or taking a walk after. I headed straight to the Cafe, trying to ignore the gray mess around. A patrol stopped me near the entrance. I'd got my papers in order. Fake, but in order. The bloke put the sheet close to his face as if he were sniffing the big, round stamp.

The Cafe's hall was bright. An enormous chandelier hung from the ceiling, giving light from the chain of electric bulbs. I approached a porter in uniform beside the heavy red curtain covering the restaurant entrance. Pulling out a tenner, I made sure he would spot it. The bloke grinned at me. The message was received.

"Good day, sir. How can I help you, sir?"

"I'm looking for Lena," I said, keeping my hand close to his.

He grabbed the bill. No one could've noticed it. His movement was admirably fast.

"I'm sorry, sir, I'm unaware of the lady you are looking for."

"Then, you should return the bill before I break all your fingers."

"Oh, sir." He chuckled. "No need for a savage action. Please follow me to the small bar. You can have your coffee and a cake there." He stretched his hand, bowing for a moment, and stepped forward.

I strolled behind him toward the glass door on the side wall. He opened one door, holding it for me to pass through. The small bar was dark, lit only by the daylight from the half-blinded windows. Not a soul inside. The door slammed closed, and he grabbed my arm, turning me to face him.

"Who the hell sent you here?!" His voice hissed. The grin disappeared, replaced by eyebrows drawn together.

"Your grandma," I said in a calm voice, taking another bill out of my pocket. "Do you want the money or not?"

His eyes jumped from side to side.

"Look, I don't have the entire day." I returned the bill and stretched my hand toward him. My fluttering fingers asked for that first tenner.

"Wait here!" He pointed to the place in the corner and disappeared, undoing the golden strap on the red curtains hanging on the side of the glass door. The curtains spread, and the room got darker.

I walked to the counter. The bar stools were heavy and couldn't be moved. A couple of glass ashtrays lay on the countertop. I stood between the bar stool where the gap was wide enough and put two ashtrays on each side, leaning my back against the polished wood. The battlefield was prepared.

The glass door opened. A young girl stepped in and walked toward me. She was small, smaller than me, putting her feet forward in a straight line. Her pastel-colored dress was simple, with no decorations. A small white top hat adorned with a small bunch of feathers rested on her head.

"I'm Lena," she said with a wide grin. "Let's go upstairs."

"That would be a pleasure, believe me. I'm not here for that, though," I said.

"We can't do it here." She giggled. "But I've always wanted to."

"You're not listening, lady. I'm not here to buy your services. I'm here to ask you some questions about Suus."

She winced.

"You're a …"

"No, I'm not a copper. And I don't want to waste your or my time, so I'm gonna make myself clear…"

The door, hidden in the shadow, burst open, and the porter rushed toward us.

"Get away from her and leave!" he said, waving his hands. I felt like Don Quixote for a moment, but instead of chasing the windmill, the windmill was chasing me.

I reached out and grabbed the ashtray, waiting for him to get closer. He stood before me with his hands in a boxing position. I grinned and winked at him, throwing the ashtray with all my strength. The bloke jerked his head to one side, but it wasn't enough. The heavy piece of glass hit him hard on the shoulder. He squeezed it, hissing in pain. I kicked him in his exposed abdomen, and the porter fell to the floor.

Lena stood there and shivered, biting her fingers covered with long white gloves.

"Now that we've clarified our relationship, I'd like to continue," I said. "I'm not here because of your business. I don't care what you two are doing. But you will tell me everything you know about Suus Achter."

Lena remained frozen. I didn't believe she had witnessed violence often. Her customers must be from higher society. How much could she ask?

The porter stood slowly up, pressing one hand against his abdomen. He climbed on the bar stool. His face wrinkled in pain. Lena leaned closer to him, rubbing his back.

"He'll be all right, don't worry. But now, tell me about you and Suus."

"Let her be. I'll tell you. What do you want to know?" the porter said.

"Oh, all right then. Tell me, how often did Suus come here? Was she your girl?"

"No. I'm only with Lena."

"Go on."

"She came here one night and brought a group of men. Lena helped her, and since then, they've worked together whenever possible. Suus was a magnet for customers," he said, stroking his tummy.

"So, you used her to expand your business, right?"

"I never took a penny from her!"

"I didn't say you did. Was she here every night?"

"No. Sometimes, she went somewhere else."

"Where?"

"I don't know." The porter lit a cigarette.

I leaned forward. "Where?!"

"I really don't know!"

Lena went behind the counter and poured a shot of Scotch. The porter nodded. She poured another one and slid it toward me. It tasted good. I should come here more often.

"I heard about a bald man who was supposed to come here regularly. Do you know him?" I said.

"There are many bald men in this cafe."

"I'm thinking of the one who could be connected to the business you're providing."

"I can't remember any bald man being with Lena."

"No, I don't mean a customer. Perhaps as competition."

"I'm the only one here."

"Tickle that walnut you have in the head a bit, please." I grinned.

"I said, I'm the only one here. From time to time, Wagner comes to find a new girl for his business. But I'd never allow Lena to work for him."

"Wagner?"

"Jonas Wagner. The pimp who works for Nazi officers."

"What with him?"

The porter spilled everything. Jonas Wagner, a German who arrived in Amsterdam right after the occupation, had started a brothel for Nazi officers in his house. He got plenty of support from the treacherous mayor Edward Vinke and was a good fella to Felix Lehmann, the right hand and secretary of *SS-Oberführer* Fabian Rausser. Yes, the head of the SS in Amsterdam. It sounded like a political game, but it was merely a private business paid from the SS piggybank held by Lehmann.

"That's very interesting. Where is his house?" I said.

"At the edge of Amsterdam on the road to Maarseen. It has a high wall around."

"I have something to say," Lena said.

We both looked at her. This was the first time she'd spoken after the incident.

"My ex-boyfriend works there. He's a waiter."

"Which one?" the porter said.

"Sami. Samuel." Her voice was low, and the porter sighed.

"Who's Sami?" I said, skipping my gaze from one to another.

"Her ex I don't like to hear about," the porter said.

"Let her speak. Why did you mention Sami?"

"I met Sami two days ago. He asked whether I knew waiters who would like to work for the Nazis. I said no."

"And?"

"If you accept, you can go there and see…"

I shook my hand to stop her. "Why the hell would I go there?"

The porter took a drag from the cigarette and blew a dense cloud of smoke over the bar counter.

"Wagner is bald."

Chapter 6

Sami appeared to be a funny bloke, always smiling, always making jokes. He was getting on my nerves. A great pal for a splendid chap like me and other bullshit. I spotted what he was up to right away. If I took the job, he would get a tick provision. I needed him, though, so I stayed with him for the rest of the day, paying for a late lunch at the diner where he liked to eat. And he liked to eat a lot. In the evening, he drove us to Wagner's house, where we were welcomed by the Nazi guards at the gate. The guards knew Sami and let us pass. He introduced me to Mr. Peters, the boss responsible for the kitchen and servers in Wagner's house.

Mr. Peters was a stout man, always complaining about people and shaking his head about why they didn't want to work for Nazis. The wage was great, and the money was the money; didn't matter where it came from. I let him talk and put his name on my list of not-to-trust people with a note about him selling his soul.

He was more than satisfied that I spoke German fluently. Although he didn't like the idea of me swaying with a tray among the Nazi officers without training. Not only could I spill drinks, but I could behave incorrectly when hearing or seeing things. My ears should be deaf, my eyes blind. That required training by him. But he agreed with me being in the kitchen. Despite me showing my skill in making scrambled eggs, he decided that it would be best if I washed dishes. I agreed, pretending endless happiness. I was in.

Everything proved the porter had been telling the truth. Wagner was a Nazi pimp. The guarded house, the fully functional kitchen, dozens of bedrooms upstairs. This degenerate threw parties *par excellence* for high-ranking Nazi officers and collaborators who profited from the system. I hadn't seen the girls yet, but my 'new colleagues' mentioned them several times. The thought of Doortje among them scared me.

The dishes rattled, and a couple of plates fell to the floor, smashing into a million pieces. Voices screaming, swearing. Heavy boots rumbled over the front kitchen where the cooks portioned the food on the plates. More swearing.

We all jumped to our feet, asking each other what happened as if there was one among us who might have had a crystal ball and know. Before we got to the swinging door leading to the dancing hall, a tall man with well-developed musculature appeared in the narrowed space splitting the kitchen in two parts and called us to gather in the front kitchen.

Four more men spread us around the space where a man was lying on the floor, bent double and hugging his knees. White shards scattered around him. The exit door swung open, and a man entered. He was about my height, wearing a dark suit, a white shirt, and a black tie. His head was bald. Jonas Wagner himself. He strode to the man on the floor and kicked him hard in the back with his polished shoe. The man made a raspy sound but remained bent double.

"Who knows this bastard?!" Wagner said, pointing at the man.

Everybody stopped breathing, avoiding looking directly at him.

"You don't know? I will show you who he is!" He turned to the man. "Take out what you have in pockets!"

The man didn't move. Wagner kicked him again, yelling his order. The man stuck his hand into a pocket and pulled out a pack of cigarettes. Wagner bent and grabbed the pack, turning around and showing it to each of us.

"See?! He stole cigarettes!"

"Those are my cigarettes. I bought them in the morning," the man said in a low, sad voice.

"This morning?!" Wagner handed the pack to the nearest waiter. "Read what's written there!"

The bloke was too intimidated or couldn't read. He stumbled over the words. Wagner got pissed and slapped him. He took the cigarettes and gave them to the next waiter. This one got a hint of bravery. He read.

"Twenty-five German cigarettes."

"German cigarettes!" said Wagner and twisted at the man on the floor again. "Did you listen, you bastard! German cigarettes! Where in the Netherlands can you buy German cigarettes?! Where?!" He kicked the man again and again until it released his anger.

"That piece of shit lies right to my eyes," he said to his gorillas, who observed the situation as if they were watching the movie in the cinema while eating popcorn. "I pay big money for having the cigarettes right from the Reich, and this piece of shit lies right to my eyes!" He kicked him one more time and glanced at us.

"Now, listen carefully, you all! You'll stay here and watch, so you'll remember the day when this piece of shit was stealing from Jonas Wagner!"

He pointed at Mr. Peters, who stood there green and unable to swallow. "And it counts to you as well. You'll bring a thief here one more time, and you'll take his place!"

Wagner spat on the floor and left.

We had to watch the torture. I'd gone through many things in my life. I'd heard a lion shrieking while being stamped by an elephant. I'd seen a wounded man being torn to pieces by angry water buffaloes. There had been nothing that could've compared to the piercing screaming of this poor man.

Chapter 7

The party was on. Officers in uniforms. Girls in thin, narrow-waisted robes. All dancing, drinking, and taking drugs hidden in the shadows. For a few moments, I imagined having a grenade, tossing it between them, and running away. I didn't have one, though.

I washed the dishes without paying attention to what I was doing. No one bothered to check. The plate was thrown into the bin if it wasn't clean enough. Otherwise, it served food with the remains of sauces, potato mash, or whatever from the previous course. The two-faced way of thinking so natural for enslaved people. Taking money, but shitting on the hand that was giving it. Hypocritical, though.

The old cook called me aside to help him strain potatoes.

"Why did you accept this job?" I said, holding the strainer with both hands.

"I have twelve small children," he said, winking at me.

"Twelve?" He could've been sixty or sixty-five years old.

"Yes, with ten women." Another wink.

I laughed and returned to the sink to continue pretending how busy I was. One more pile of dirty plates, and I would sneak to the door to observe guests one more time.

The cook approached and took me by the sleeve, pulling me to the back of the kitchen.

"Look," he said, showing me a bottle with a brown substance.

"What's that?" I said.

"A bromide."

"A bromide?"

"Shhh!" He leaned closer. "I pour it into the soup and sauces. To get their little worms lazy."

"But it…" He pulled my arm with such a strength that I bent over.

"But it hasn't been proved it works," I whispered.

"The British gave it to their soldiers during the first war so that they wouldn't think about women."

"I've heard that, all right. But no one's ever said it really curbed the sexual urge."

"I did. After my soup, they can't write with their pens. And know you what? They praise my soup." He chuckled. "I must cook it almost every night. They are crazy about it."

"Why are you doing it?"

"Why? I don't want them to fornicate with our girls. Filthy pigs. I hate them." He spat on the floor. "I'm getting it from a friend of mine who works in a pharmacy. Sometimes, he doesn't have enough bromide, and then he gives me sleeping pills. Last time, the entire party slept five minutes before eleven. That was the best night here."

I laughed. Hard to believe his idea worked, but it was kinda lovable. I couldn't forget he came here for money in the first place, though.

I went to the door and peered through the small round window. A massive crystal chandelier with hundreds of lights lit the dance hall as if it was the sun. Perhaps not hundreds. The light reflected from crystal trimmings across the entire color spectrum. It hurt my eyes. The only shadow was under the gallery. Everybody was twisting around, dancing to the brisk rhythm of the waltz. And then I spotted her. She stood there alone, wearing a simple pastel green dress. Doortje Smit. I put the stained white apron down and sneaked out of the kitchen. Swinging around the dancing pairs, I got closer to her and caught her hand.

Doortje gazed at me and grinned. Her smile was slow and hazy as if it came through a long-distance call. She swayed and put her hand around my neck, thinking I was her new dancing partner. That bastard drugged her. Her pupils were widened, and her eyes glared like the two headlights of an automobile.

Holding her hand, I pulled her away, heading back to the kitchen and keeping as close to the walls as possible. We reached the swinging door. I opened it and pushed her in. The kitchen had a back door for supplies. Perfect for running away unspotted. I grabbed an old winter coat the cooks used when they went to the food storage in the cellar and wrapped her in it.

"What are you doing?" she said in a dreamy voice, grinning like a stoner.

"I'm taking you back to your father," I whispered.

"No. I don't want to go to Argentina." Her foot stamped down.

"Shhh. Don't worry. Everything will be all right." I wrapped my hands around her shoulders, nudging her away.

"No, I don't. What did you put on my new dress?" She raised her voice. "Eww, it stinks!"

"Shhh! We need to hurry. Be quiet."

"I don't want to be quiet. I've been quiet for a long time," she said and jerked from my hug. For a moment, she just stared and then cried. Big tears fell down her cheeks, and she sobbed.

"Shhh! Don't cry. Please."

She couldn't stop. Panic caught her, shaking her body like she had touched an electric wire connected to the socket.

Perhaps it was the drugs. I didn't know. I slapped her cheeks. Strong enough to stop her crying.

Her eyes turned to two angry flames. "Why did you slap me?"

"I didn't want to. I'm sorry."

"Why did you slap me?!" She thrust me back with such force that I lost my balance and fell on the floor. What the hell they had given her?

The door slammed open, and Wagner entered, striding, followed by Sami.

"That's him!" Sami said, pointing his finger at me. "See? I've told you. He wanted to sabotage your party and kidnap this prostitute."

"Sami, what the hell are you doing?" I said.

"Shut up! I won't lose my job because of you!"

"Fucking toady!" I slapped him hard.

Sami covered his cheek with his palm, retreating from me.

Wagner observed what was happening without saying a word. His gorillas appeared. He pointed at me.

"Seize him! And take the girl back to the room!"

Chapter 8

The small room had no windows. The weak light of the bare bulb spread around, making everything yellow. There was nothing but a wooden chair. I sat on it, surrounded by five men. They wore the same black suits, the same white shirts, and had the same stone faces. Their arms were enormous, as were their chests. One could've cycled around such a chest. I took a deep breath, but my lungs protested. The air was heavy and full of damp.

Wagner paced in circles between me and his five gorillas. It would be a jolly evening among friends if it went like this. Perhaps I should ask for a shot of Scotch.

"Who are you?" Wagner said, still circling.

"I'm Erik, your new employee."

"Don't bullshit me, man!"

"You asked, I answered."

Wanger stopped and nodded at one gorilla. The mountain of muscles stepped closer and slapped me hard. In an instant, I found myself lying on the floor. I expected my cheek to burn, but it didn't. There was no cheek at all. I pressed my tongue to the spot where it was supposed to be. The tongue found something, but that something didn't feel the tongue.

Another pair of hands grabbed me, and the hard wooden seat pressed into my buttocks again. Wagner stared at me. His face asked questions I didn't understand.

"We can continue like this if you want," he said.

"Yeah? It was fun. Can we do it again?" I said.

"A hero!" Wagner chuckled and nodded again.

This one came from behind, this time changing the direction. I fell on the other side. The floor was dirty and cold. A little angel rang a bell in my ears.

"Would you put some carpet on the floor or clean it, please? I don't want to get eczema," I said, sitting again on the chair. My head spun slowly.

"Let him be!" Wagner said, waving his hand at the gorilla standing before me and stepping closer. "Now, young man, it's time to sing. Let me hear your song."

"Believe me, you wouldn't want to hear me singing. I was banned even from the school choir."

"Do you know that I can get you killed? And nothing will happen to me. Do you know that?"

"I think I do."

"Then, tell me, what's your name?"

"I said. I'm Erik."

"Erik who?"

"Erik Müller."

"And why was you pulling that girl out, *Herr* Müller?"

"She's my sister."

"Sister? Did you hear that?" He turned to the gorillas. "Erik Müller came for his sister! His mom sent him because she was late for dinner."

The gorillas laughed. The same tone, the same pitch, and rhythm. They must have practiced a lot.

My cheeks returned to their places, and my face burned like hell.

"Bring that waiter!" Wagner said.

One gorilla marched toward the door and opened it, bending when passing through. After a couple of seconds, he returned with Sami, leading him by the shoulder with his hand the size of an excavator's shovel.

"Who is this man?" Wagner said, pointing at me.

"He's Erik Jansen."

"And what is he doing?"

"He's a private detective."

"How do you know that?"

"My ex-girlfriend told me."

Wagner turned to me. "So, what do you say now?"

I said nothing because there was nothing to say. The idiot seized the opportunity to lick this man's boots, and I was about to pay his bill.

"Make him talk!"

The gorilla standing before me swung his arm, hitting me straight under my nose with his fist. The chair tilted back and, taking its time as if it was deciding whether or not to fall, went down, taking me with it. I lost vision for a few seconds. The taste of iron splashed over my mouth. My lips swelled, and the angel exchanged the bell for a drum. Someone lifted me.

"Talk!"

"All right. I'm a private detective," I said, trying not to fall off the chair.

"Why are you here?"

"I told you already. The girl's my sister."

"What's her name?"

"Doortje."

Wagner gazed at the bloke beside him. The gorilla nodded.

"Your sister is a hooker?"

"What's wrong with being a hooker? Your house is full of them."

"Not a good one, though. She doesn't want to work."

"That's why I'm here. To solve your problem."

"Wasn't it you who talked to that prostitute yesterday evening?" he said, scratching his chin. "Wasn't it him?"

The asked gorilla nodded. "Looks like him. She said some name when I beat her."

"What name?"

The gorilla shrugged, and Wagner waved his hand. "I didn't expect anything else."

"You killed Suus?!" I said.

"What do you think?" Wagner said, grinning at me. "I don't allow a dirty hooker to ruin my business. He killed her, and I tipped off the police."

I said nothing. They were all connected.

"Beat him! And throw him somewhere. I don't want to see his face again." He turned away.

"Mr. Wagner, thank you for the opportunity. I'd like to work with you more," Sami said, reaching out with his hand.

"And who are you?" Wagner said, ignoring the outstretched hand.

"Sami. My name is Sami."

"And where's your place?" Wagner said and walked toward the door.

Sami spun, following Wagner. "I'm a waiter, but I want to be more. I want to work for you, not for Mr. Peters."

Wagner stopped and gazed at him. "You won't," he said and moved again.

"But, I thought I had proven my loyalty."

Wagner twisted on the spot, flames in his eyes. "You? Do you think I would work with a dirty rat? A stool pigeon who might betray me one day? Shit willingly on my reputation?"

Sami stepped back, raising his hands. "I'm not a rat. I believe I deserve your trust. It was me who told you about Erik."

"You deserve? Let me show you what you deserve."

Like the wave of a magic wand, a Luger appeared in his hand. He pointed it at Sami and pulled the trigger. Sami jerked backward, his mouth dropping open, body falling to the floor. A crimson dot in the middle of his forehead. A blood pool developed under his head.

"Clean it!" he said, nodding at the one gorilla.

Then he walked to the door. When he grasped the door handle, he turned. "Make him suffer!" he said and left.

The gorillas stepped closer, grinning.

"Boys! Perhaps we can have some Scotch and play cards afterward, what do you reckon?" I said, raising my hands.

I got one from the right and another from the left. They tossed me between them like a rag doll stolen from a little girl. The chair flew away, and I reached the ground level. The gorillas put their legs into action.

This could've been a lovely evening full of friendly chitchat. My consciousness said something about taking a day off. The room hazed, then darkened.

Chapter 9

The coldness pierced my skin. I shivered and opened my eyes. Darkness covered everything. My body hurt. I lay on my back. Every spot in contact with a hard surface sent bunches of pain to my brain. I tried to move my hands, but it hurt more, so I gave up. The last thing I remembered was them beating me, but I didn't remember who they had been. I didn't remember why I'd been there, and I didn't remember where I had been.

Steps reverberated through the air. Someone was coming. Any attempts to move and turn my head ended up in more pain. I just lay, waiting for him or her to approach. The breathing got sharper contours. A man. He huffed like a bear; he must have been old.

A shadow leaned over me, but I didn't see the face. Something poked me. I coughed, but the burst of a new pain stopped me.

"Who the hell are you?" the man said.

I tried to answer, to tell him, to ask him for help. I had no energy.

Something clanged. Two hands grabbed me and pulled me, making me want to scream. The coldness of a metal surface replaced the cold ground. More pain. It struck my brain, and I fainted again.

I woke up in a bed, covered by an ancient brown blanket. My body still hurt, but less than I remembered the last time. The room was small, warm, and smelled of ginger. The sun winked at me from behind the small window. In the corner stood an old stove with a pot on it. Steam rose. I heard water simmering.

The door opened, and an old man stepped in. He could be a hundred years old, bent by the weight of his age. His face was unshaven. He carried a bunch of wood, hugging it with his wrinkled hands.

"Ah, there you are," he said and dumped the wood on the floor near the stove.

"How did you sleep?"

I tried to say something, but my throat deceived me, making a growling noise.

"Wait, don't talk."

The man approached, stuck his hand under the pillow, and lifted my head. With his other hand, he put a cup with warm liquid on my lips. I sipped. Tea with ginger and honey. Even a lemon. It felt good, and I sipped more. A bottomless thirst seized my mind. I opened my mouth more, and tea splashed down my chin.

"Slowly, man." He grinned. "You'll choke yourself."

He put my head back on the pillow. "I made bone broth. That will help you better."

Wobbling a bit, he paced toward the stove, taking another cup from the table in the middle of the room. He stirred the broth in the pot and poured a portion into the cup with a gigantic white scoop.

The ginger tea warmed my body. I felt the energy flowing through my veins. I sat up on the bed, leaning against my hands. It hurt, but it was bearable.

"I found you in the woods, carried you here, washed you," the old man said, wobbling back to the bed. "You were painted in blood and had a few ribs cracked. Since I moved here, I've found five people lying on the ground. You're the sixth one."

He handed me the cup. The broth smelled like never before. I took a sip. Not too hot, not too cold. It even tasted like never before, reminding me of my mother treating me with broth when I'd been ill. Perhaps a pinch of salt was missing, but I was grateful for what I got, slurping, and swallowing it.

"I buried them in the woods where it opens to a small meadow. Those poor men deserved better, but I couldn't carry them into the cemetery. You're the first one I found alive."

"Thank you," I said in a weak voice, handing him the empty cup.

"One more?"

I nodded.

"Who are you?" he said, pouring the new portion.

"Erik. Erik Jansen." My voice was still weak, clawing my throat as if I'd swallowed nails.

The man reappeared at the bed, handed me the cup, and sat on the chair waiting nearby.

"I'm Nicolaes Claasen," he said.

"I know you."

"You do?"

"You're a teacher."

"I was a teacher, indeed."

"You taught in our school. I remember you living by Vondelpark in that small fancy building. You disappeared when they came."

"Disappeared? Not exactly. I just moved here."

"Why?"

"I'm *persona non grata*."

"Unwanted person?"

"Indeed. I printed local newspapers. It was my hobby. I've always dreamed about being a journalist," he said and fell into the thoughts.

"I think I remember the newspapers. Each issue had a sun printed on the front page."

He nodded. "But the Nazis didn't like it. They banned all newspapers in the country and murdered many owners." His voice saddened, taking him into thoughts again.

Suddenly, he slapped his leg. "So, I ran away. I'm not a hero." He grinned. "At least not when it comes to torture during interrogation."

I returned the grin. "When did you find me?"

"You've been laying in my bed for two days."

"Two days?"

He nodded. "Exactly. Do you want to tell me what happened?"

I told him everything but Mr. Smit. Doortje became once again my sister. He listened with both ears to my story, sometimes nodding, sometimes coughing, or scratching his back.

"That's unbelievable," he said. "For my entire life, my most exciting adventure was when I caught students smoking behind the corner of the school. It was so thrilling, that I forgot to tell about them to the school director."

I laughed. He hadn't been teaching me, but he had an excellent reputation among the students. Now I knew why. He saw human beings, not students.

"What are you going to do now?"

"I don't know. I want to make up for you for saving my life."

He raised his hands. "Don't even think about it! You gave me an opportunity to feel something I thought I lost forever."

"What?"

"A pleasure of celebrating the life. I've buried five men. But not you, and that counts for me more than anything else."

"Thank you, Mr. Claasen!" I said.

"Oh, come on! Don't mention it anymore. Especially not in front of Nazis."

I nodded.

"So, what will you do next? Are you going back to take your sister away?"

"No, I don't think so."

"Come on! You won't let them harm her! That's not how I know you."

"You don't know me."

"I think I remember you from the school. And your sister as well. You were a little fella who fought with everyone who bullied the weaker kids."

He remembered it well. That had been me. This enemy was stronger, though. Way stronger than a bunch of teenage kids. I couldn't fight with him. He'd secured his power thoroughly. I would go, find Mr. Smit, and return all the money he had given me.

"I'll show you something. Do you think you can walk?"

I tried. My muscles were stiff, and it took a lot of pain to make them work again. But I could move. One bright light in the endless darkness.

The old man led me to the back room. It had no windows and stank of something I didn't recognize. A machine stood in the middle, taking up almost the entire space. Black stains splashed everywhere. And piles of paper sheets. I checked one out. And grinned.

It was a flyer with words imprinted in big letters "*Death to Nazis! Kill 'em all! Freedom!*" I'd seen this flyer before.

"That's my way of fighting against the oppressors. I'm too old to pick up a gun and shoot them. So, I'm doing this."

"How do you distribute them?"

"I'd like to tell you, but I don't. I'm risking a lot just by showing you this printing press. If the Gestapo or the SS caught you, they would get it out of you quickly."

I nodded. The old man was right.

"But why did you show me this."

"Maybe I'm stupid, but I wanted to encourage you not to give up!" He pierced me with his gaze. "And I can tell it worked. I see flames in your eyes." And gave me a big smile.

Chapter 10

"I have no idea what to do," I said.

We returned to the kitchen and sat at the table. Nicholaes had made more ginger tea, but now, he poured in a dose of Jenever. I'd have rather gone with Scotch, but somehow, the local gin went along with the ginger tea.

"How many flyers did you print so far?"

"Many. I don't count them."

"Can you change the text?"

"Anytime."

"How long does it take?"

"No longer than twenty-four hours. I need to etch the new text to the cylinder. Why are you asking?"

"I'm just curious," I said, sipping tea.

We sat there, each immersed in his thoughts. The tick of the clock hanging on the wall became louder. A fly flew across the room. The buzzing tore ears. It landed on the window.

"Will you return there?" Nicolaes said.

"Not yet. No way to do so. Not now."

"You must find a way how to sneak in unnoticed."

"Yeah, I know."

"You can't be disguised as a waiter anymore."

"Yeah, I know."

"Maybe you can dress up like a hooker."

"Yeah, I kn… No, I can't. Girls wear thin, light clothes. Even if I shaved my chest, they still would see I'm a man."

"They'll be drunk."

I shook my head.

The fly took off again, flying around my and Nicholaes' head and torturing us with an unbearable buzzing. I waved my hand, but it flew away, mocking me by landing on my head. I tapped myself. No success. The cheeky fly left without giving a shit.

Nicholaes strolled toward the cupboard and took out a sugar cube and a long, narrow glass. He put the sugar in the middle of the table and waited, the glass prepared in his hand.

"I'll try to find someone who's insane enough to go there with me and shoot them all," I said.

"It would be considered extremely foolish to proceed with that course of action."

"Why?"

"Come on! You know. You said there were guards."

"A few soldiers. They are nothing compared to the five gorillas. Those blokes are trained assassins."

"Quite a lot of people with guns, don't you reckon?"

I nodded. I knew he was right. Just needed to say something.

"But you could set a couple of bombs there."

"No. That would kill my sister as well. And there's no guarantee they will die. They could be wounded. And I don't have a source on bombs."

He nodded.

The fly had found a partner. Now, they flew together in the space between the table and the lamp hanging from the ceiling, creating spectacular curves in the air. It was a dance a human would never be capable of dancing.

"This silence is killing me," I said and stood up.

Nicholaes poured more tea into the cups. He grabbed the Jenever bottle and filled each cup to the top, using just one hand, still holding the long glass.

"Why do you hold that glass?"

"You'll see."

I paced around the room. My powerlessness pissed me off. I didn't believe they had all the power in the world. They looked strong, but they were just people who had desires and made mistakes. *Think, Erik, there must be a weak point!*

Two flies succumbed to the temptation of the sugar and landed right on the sweet cube. Nicholaes inched the glass toward them. The sugar weakened their vigilance because they didn't pay attention to what was happening around them. The old man darted his hand, but the insects flew away. He moved the sugar cube closer and waited, keeping the hand with the glass nearby. After a few seconds, both flies landed on the sugar again. A brief movement, and he trapped both flies under the glass.

"Aha! Gotcha!" he said, rubbing his palms.

I stopped at the table. Two flies circled the wall of the glass, flying around or walking on it. They realized they'd been trapped and desperately fought for their lives. Sugar was no longer the number one for them.

"That's how you should treat every bitch who irritates you. By setting the trap for them. Offer something they crave for, and you can do what you want with them."

I grinned at him. "You're still a teacher."

"Old habits are dying for a long time."

"I wish I could set a trap…"

"What?"

But I waved my hands, leaving him stunned by his hunting success, and paced around the room again, chafing my feet. I had never known why, but it helped me to think.

"Well, I hope you won't make a hole into the floor." Those were the last words I heard.

A trap! What a magical word. Set a trap; get rid of him. But how to set it? Nicholaes had offered something the flies hadn't had but wanted. What could I offer to Wagner? Money? He swam in money. Money wouldn't lead him away. Power? I remembered how he'd shot Sami. His power was stronger at his house. Even offering hookers wouldn't work. He has a house full of them.

I stopped pacing and gazed at the glass with trapped flies. What trap would it be?

I couldn't offer something Wagner hadn't had. Could I take something from him? Money? No. Neither power nor hookers. He had plenty, and all protected by trained soldiers. Could I take something he protected less? Like his car or wife. A favorite dog. Did he have a wife or a dog? I could take his life, shooting from a distance. That idea made me feel good, but it would solve nothing. His death didn't mean Doortje would be free. I could take his reputation by... *Holy crap!*

Chapter 11

I returned to the table and sat on the chair.

"Nicholaes, how many flyers have you printed so far?"

"Around five hundred."

"I will need them all."

"All? Are you going to burn something?" he said, tapping on the glass.

"Yes, but not literally."

"What are you up to? Tell the old man."

"Look, could I take Wagner's life?"

"Yes, but it would cost you your life."

"Could I take his money, house, or other possessions?"

He shook his head. "I guess, no."

"What else could I take?"

Nicholaes shrugged. "I don't know."

"His reputation."

"Reputation? What reputation does he have? He's a scoundrel."

"He, dear Nicholaes, has a successful reputation when we look through his eyes. He has perfect relations with the mayor, Edward Vinke…"

We both spat on the floor.

"He has excellent relations with the head of the SS. He's trusted."

"So?"

"Let's make him untrustworthy."

"How?"

"We… No, I slip your flyers into his house. And the printing press. Then I tip the SS off. It will look like he's agitating against them. You know what's the punishment for this?"

"A bullet to the head. How will you do that?"

"What? Placing the flyers?"

"No. To install the printing press. It weighs tons. I needed ten men to move it here. And a heavy truck."

"I didn't say my plan is perfect. It has bugs, but bugs can be fixed. At least, it's a plan."

He grinned. "Yeah, sounds like a plan. And I think it's a good plan. I'm proud of you, Erik. Why didn't I teach you? Or I did? The old man doesn't remember."

"No, you didn't. That's not important, though. Let's focus on the plan. Could flyers only be enough?"

Nicholaes put his finger on his chin. "No," he said after a while. "He can say it was a sabotage. Because he has an, you said, excellent relation with the head of the SS, they will believe him."

"Then we need to figure out how to get your printing press there."

"No, not at all," he said, shaking his head.

"Why not?"

"Because I have only this one. And it wasn't cheap. And what will I do after? How will I print more flyers?"

"You won't."

"Come one! You can take the only pleasure from an old man!"

"It's the higher interest."

"Shit on your higher interest!"

"Nicholaes, please! I'll buy you another one. Better. Bigger."

He laughed and tapped his thighs. "I'm sorry, Erik. I was just teasing you."

"Oh, that's so nice of you. I'm stuck, and mister teacher is making fun of me," I said, grinning. "So, how do we find the truck and load it with the press?"

"No, we don't."

"Again? You're a jolly old man."

"We don't need to." He stood up. "Wait here," he said and walked again toward the door to the next room with the press.

At the door, he turned to me. "Don't drink the entire Jenever. It's the last bottle I have. Wait for me."

"I didn't intend to."

He came back, carrying a heavy metal box. Panting, he put it on the table.

"Open it!"

I did. It was full of short metal square sticks sorted in small sections of the box. Each stick had a flat end, and on each end was a letter.

"My old movable type. I used it for the early versions of my newspapers," he said with pride in his voice.

"And?"

"I have a small manual press. I don't need it. You can bring it to Wagner's house. It's mostly wooden, so the weight won't be a problem."

I checked each section, pulling the sticks out. A, B, C, D, E, F.

"But this is not complete. Letters are missing."

"They are not missing. They are in the room. You couldn't expect an old man to carry all those heavy boxes here?"

"But aren't they too heavy to bring them there?"

"Oh, now you care about the weight." He grinned. "Yes, they are heavy but lighter than the big printing press. You're young and strong."

"Sounds good to me. How far away is Wagner's house from here?"

"Around 20 kilometers."

"Crap! Another problem to solve."

"No. This problem is already solved. I have a car," he said.

"But…"

"No, there will be no problem. I have a permit from the SS office to use the car. And gasoline too."

"But it's on your name and your birth date?"

"Do you think I asked for it from the gendarmery? I'll make one in your name."

I shook my head, impressed by the old teacher. This man ruled. "We should load the car now."

"Slowly, young man. First, we need to print new flyers."

"Why?"

"The movable type has a different font as does the printing press. You need the flyers to be authentic, don't you?"

"How much time it will take?"

"The hardest part is to set the matrix. The pressing is easy."

I stood up.

"Let's press those things, old man!"

"Yeah, young man! Let's do it. We have all night."

I winced.

"Don't worry, I lied. I have two more bottles of Jenever."

* * *

I sat in Nicholaes' old Ford and observed the gate, hidden behind the bush on the opposite side of the road, and waited for an opportunity to sneak in. The car was old, one of the first models imported to Europe. It had a hand-crank for starting the engine. The darkness of the night disappeared, and the sky was getting brighter and brighter from the sun hidden behind the horizon. The air smelled of pines, carrying the dump from the sea, and was cold. I appreciated it. My body hurt like hell. The coldness helped to reduce the pain. Jumping around the printing press took its price. It would take weeks to recover.

We'd worked almost the entire night. The first hour had been a total disaster, but then we'd synchronized, and the flyers had piled up. Only small incidents had interrupted the work, like drinking, peeing, or my stupidity when I'd spilled the printing ink by accident. All five hundred flyers were packed in a small rucksack. The wooden printing press was bound to it. I could run with it on my back if my body didn't hurt. The entire package weighed around forty pounds.

Wagner must have thrown another party. Cars were leaving the house in small groups or solo. The guards closed the gate. My time had come.

I got out of the car, hissing from the pain, and put the rucksack on my back. The sharp edges pressed against my skin, making me want to throw everything on the ground. Pricking my ears, I ensured no vehicles were coming and then crossed the road.

Wagner's house wasn't just a house. It was a small castle surrounded by a park. I entered the shade under the trees, strolling along the wall. It was way too high to jump and pull up with that heavy load on my back. I cursed myself for not bringing a rope. After a few minutes, I stopped and ran my fingers over the gap between the stones cemented together in the wall. It was old and crumbled. It would take days to release the stone out of it, though. I carry on, hoping that, at some place, the wall would be damaged.

There was no end to the wall, and I was losing all my energy. The park around the house was vast. I put the rucksack down and touched the edges of the stones. No way to climb up. The edges were too narrow. I had to change the plan and try it again tomorrow, bringing a ladder and a rope. This idea sounded horrible. Who knew what those bastards had done to the Smit's daughter while I had been recovering from my wounds? A sudden anger shook my body, but clenching my fists wouldn't help.

Enough resting. I put the rucksack back and strolled on. The trees growing along the wall stood at a variable distance from it. Some closer, some farther. All high oaks and beeches with no branches at a reachable height. I turned back, decided to return tomorrow, but itching in my mind told me to go a couple more feet.

After a minute, I spotted the linden tree. Its lower branches reached above the wall, but its trunk grew at an angle, creating a slanted surface. I rushed closer. The trunk was wide enough for me to walk on it. This would do. I stepped on it, spreading my hands like a tightrope walker and bending my back to lower the gravity point. My boots slipped, and I was on the ground before I could say a word. More pressure. I needed more pressure.

I stepped on the trunk and slipped again before I put my other foot on it. The bark was rough enough. The problem was my worn shoes. Their soles were smooth like a piece of glass. I took them off, as well as the socks, put everything into the rucksack, and climbed again on the trunk. It got better, but it needed more strength.

Balancing, I reached the strong branch that led over the wall. I sat on it. My legs were shaking. After catching up on breath, I moved forward, sliding on my ass. The sweat poured in all directions, and my shirt was swimming in it.

No guards around. They must have patrolled at the gate only. Cursing like a charioteer, I jumped on the grassy ground and rolled.

The grass was wet and mowed. It didn't bother me at all. I put my shoes back and got up. I was in the meadow with a few small bushes, way deep behind the house. The strip of trees covered it. I hardly caught a glimpse. To my surprise, a few feet toward the gate stood a wooden shed. Or a barn? Didn't matter. I thanked all gods and the entire universe. No need to sneak into the house. This would do better. A hidden place where Wagner could have printed anti-Nazi flyers.

The shed was around fifty feet long and around twenty feet wide. I could reach the slanted roof at the back. A gravel road led toward the house. The shed had three doors along the wall and a separate door on the side, locked with a padlock. I looked around to find something I could stick between the door and the wall to pry it off the hinges. A peek around the corner exposed two armed Nazi soldiers striding toward the shed. Three dogs ran before them. Our gaze locked, and they began to bark like crazy.

I jumped as fast as I could at the door. Many stories had been told about trained Nazi dogs. Those creatures were dangerous. I rattled the door, hoping it would open. A waste of time; miracles didn't happen. I climbed up to the roof. It felt like pressing against a moving truck. The more I tensed my tired muscles, the slower I moved up. Fighting with panting, I lay on the roof tiles right when the dogs arrived. They jumped around the shed and barked. The lack of oxygen spun my head. That urge to take a deep breath was killing me. I put both palms over my mouth and nose and inhaled until my lungs expanded, keeping quiet. Next time, I would bring a ladder, a rope, and pieces of raw meat.

"What is going on?" a voice said in German.

"Why are you barking?" another German voice said.

The door rattled.

"Everything is locked."

The barking had no end.

"Hush! Quiet!"

"I can't see anything inside. Stop, you bastards, or I'll shoot you!"

"It must have been a squirrel. Or a rat."

"Come! Come, for God's sake!"

Something cracked, and one dog squealed. The barking changed to a muffled growl.

"Yes, the rat or a squirrel. Or a girl." The voice chuckled.

"Have you heard? They will send them away. Tonight's the last night for a lot of them. The officers are bored and need new meat."

"New meat? Bloody hell! Where are they sending them?"

"I don't know. A work camp, maybe. Come!"

Silence.

I lay still for another couple of seconds, taking shallow breaths. Then I dared to lift my head. I spotted two soldiers strolling toward the house, accompanied by dogs. I rolled over and gazed at the sky, trying to digest what I'd just overheard. Tonight. It had to be done tonight. The sun appeared over the tops of the trees.

Chapter 12

It wasn't a shed. It was a garage, dark and spacious. I'd disassembled the roof tiles, slipped in, and landed on the car's roof. Two cars, both Volkswagen Beetles, parked right next to each other. A two-wing door before each. The space behind the third door was empty. Oil stains on the concrete floor whispered that the garage harbored another car. I didn't care what it could be. The space in the corner dragged my attention.

Why fate liked me so much, I had no idea. A heavy table stood right there. What could be the best place to print the flyers? I untied the press and put it on the table. Nice. The matrix with letters had twisted a bit, but tightening the screws on the side fixed it. It fitted to the block of the press like a jigsaw puzzle. I arranged the flyers into two piles, leaving a couple of sheets scattered on the table and the floor. Many of them had blurred letters, as we hadn't paid attention to the quality during the printing. It didn't matter. They were readable. I opened the bottle with the printing ink and splashed it around. The last thing in the rucksack was a couple of metal letter sticks; I dumped them on the table.

I moved farther back and took a last glance. It looked good. A secret printing den. The SS would like it.

Now, after I got rid of the load, I felt light, like a bird. I climbed back on the car, snuck out the roof. No dogs around. No guards. I watched the surroundings for a while and put the tiles back, removing all traces. I jumped off the roof. Planks were piled at the back of the garage. I took one, strong enough to hold my weight, and leaned it against the wall. Then ran on it, jumped, and grabbed on to the top stone. No one troubled me on the way back. I was so pumped to find the hidden old Ford untouched. The gate was wide open, but no guards patrolled. Right when I was about to hop out and start the engine with a hand-crank, the noise of a coming vehicle rattled. A military truck stopped at the gate.

Ten soldiers jumped off the truck's bed and marched through the gate. Those two blokes must have called for backup. I was a lucky bastard; I had made it out in time. Would they comb through this side of the road? Perhaps I should run away. Ford could lead to Nicholaes, though. What story should I prepare if they found me? Wagner could have been present during the interrogation. He would know me. Sweat covered my forehead. I wiped it off.

Another group of soldiers strolled from the gate. They jumped on the truck's bed. The truck revved the engine and took off. The gate closed again. How could I have been so stupid? The guards changed. Of course! One squad couldn't be on duty all the time. Stupid, stupid.

I spun the hand-crank. The engine caught its breath and purred. I left for Amsterdam.

* * *

The road to Amsterdam was empty, and nobody stopped me. I parked the car at the corner near the stadium, five minutes' walk to Euterpestraat, where the SS, SD, and Gestapo had headquarters. The streets weren't busy. The city was waking up to the new day. A couple of patrols strolled, with tired faces. They must have been a morning shift, which meant getting out of bed too early.

I took out a flyer I'd kept in the glove box. Nicholaes had given me a pencil to write a brief message for the SS. I did so on the back of the flyer.

"This flyer was printed by Jonas Wagner. The printing press is hidden in the corner of the garage behind his house."

Short and exact. Enough, though. A long anonymous letter would be suspicious to skeptical Nazi heads.

The sun was shining. The air was scorching. I took off my jacket and stepped out of the car. I wouldn't need it. The lock on the door wasn't working, so I didn't bother even to pretend I was locking it. No one would have stolen this old vehicle, anyway.

I strolled toward Euterpestraat. The headquarters were in a three-story building. I remembered it had been a school. The Nazis took everything that they liked. I passed the bakery. The bloke opened the shop's door, and the smell of freshly baked bread made my stomach twist. My life in the last couple of days was sad. A small truck passed me, making a noise that could've awakened dead people. The milk bottles rattled on its bed. Families were having breakfast. The windows were open, and the air smelled of brewed coffee.

I stood in front of the task I had no idea how to accomplish. How would I deliver the message? I couldn't send it by the post office. That idea was absurd, leading to nowhere. I couldn't hand it to someone either. They would arrest or shoot me in an instant. More and more people in uniforms passed me, rushing to the offices. An undeniable sign that I was getting closer. Their impassive faces said nothing. No one could guess what they were thinking of. Thinking was suspicious and often handed over a ticket to prison. Perhaps I could slip the flyer into someone's pocket. No. Not reliable enough.

I crossed Mivervalaan, the broad avenue with the strip of trees in the middle, running all the way from the channel and ending at a park before Apollolaan. SS headquarters was right around the corner. A bloke from the patrol stared at me. They were having coffee. I grinned and nodded. He grinned back and said something to his partner, who jerked his head. They laughed.

Two SS men guarded the entrance to the SS headquarters building. Everybody who passed them had to show a paper. No way for me. I had reliable fake papers, but that wasn't enough to get in.

"What are you doing here?" the voice said from behind.

I turned and looked at the faces of those two guards who had just drunk coffee.

"I'm heading to work," I said.

"Show you papers!"

I pulled the folded sheet from my trousers' back pocket and handed it to him.

He gazed at the letters for a while and returned it to me.

"Where do you work?"

"Fons Vitae Lyceum."

"That's where?"

I pointed my hand forward. "There."

"Why are you going this way? You could go on Apollolaan," said the other.

I shrugged.

"What are you doing in Lyceum?"

"Teaching young cooks."

"Cooks?"

"Yes. Lyceum produces the best cooks in Europe."

"I thought Lyceum was a high school."

"It is," I said.

"I'll never understand the Dutch," the first one said, and they chuckled.

"What happened to your face? Did you fight? In the pub? For a girl?" the other said.

"Yeah."

"You lost?"

"Yeah."

The bloke handed me my papers.

"Go and, next time, choose another way!"

I nodded and turned away from them. A car stopped right at the entrance. The door opened, and Jonas Wagner stepped out of the car and buttoned the jacket. Two of his gorillas followed, and they rushed to the building without paying attention to what was happening around them. Doubts caught my mind and shook it. I couldn't do it. It was too risky. I should've expected Wagner and his gorillas to be often a guest here. If he had seen my face, the consequences would have been fatal.

I waited for him to disappear and walked straight. At the corner, I turned and bumped into a man in an SS uniform.

"Hey! Careful!" he said.

"I'm sorry," I said and lifted my head. It was an SS officer.

He grinned. "No harm done. Such things happen. Are you all right?"

"Yes. Thank you."

"You look stressed, young man, and I see you were fighting. For a girl?"

"I'm sorry officer…"

"*Untersturmführer* Scholtz."

"…*Untersturmführer* Scholtz, I'm late for work."

"Oh, then I won't delay you." He stepped aside and waved his hand in a polite gesture.

A brisk idea flashed through my mind. I reached into the pocket and pulled the flyer out. Now or never. I handed it to him.

"This will be interesting for you," I said and ran.

I was at least a hundred meters away from him when I heard, "Wait! Wait! Where did you get this?!"

I didn't stop until I reached the car. Sitting behind the steering wheel, I grasped it with both hands. My heart pounded. The veins on my neck pulsed. No one followed me. For today, I was fed up with Nazis. If any of them had shown up and talked to me, I would have shot him right in the face. If I had had a gun.

Chapter 13

The truck arrived. It went straight in because they kept the gate open. I was again on the stakeout, hidden behind the bushes. The daylight weakened, and the night creatures living in the park were waking up. I'd spent the whole damned day sitting in the car, wasting the precious time. Nothing had been happening. No one had come to arrest Wagner. No one made a bust.

In the morning, I'd headed to Carl's diner after I'd run away from the officer. Carl had made me my usual scrambled eggs and coffee. Smiling, he'd mentioned Mr. Smit. To my immense relief, the old man was all right and back to his hideout. He had left for food right when I'd been looking for him. Carl had recommended me to Mr. Smit.

More and more trucks. One parked before the gate. I saw blokes unloading bottles, halves of pig carcasses, and crates with vegetables. Filthy Nazi high-society ready to get drunk and harass young, drugged girls who had no hopes of running away and saving their lives and dignity. And then sent them to their deaths. New meat! Disgusting.

Another truck arrived. The same one I'd seen in the morning. The soldiers got in, and it left. Strange, though. They took the guards away without exchanging them for a fresh squad. The gate closed. Perhaps another truck would bring them. Or maybe they didn't want to be guarded anymore. The last night, they had said. I had enough. Needed to sneak in. I got out of the car. Doortje had to be dragged away from this nest of lust. Now.

A heavy cloud spread in the sky, and a wind began to blow from the sea. Cold and damp. I jogged to the spot with the linden tree. It was waiting for me. It felt like meeting an old friend. I climbed over the wall. The darkness hugged the space, and I darted toward the house, crouching and hiding behind the bushes. A dog barking echoed in the distance. Cursing the idea of coming here without a piece of meat, I approached the house's walls and prayed to be unnoticed by those four-legged bastards.

One window on the first floor, a foot and something above the ground, was ajar. I pushed it open and gazed in, standing on my toes and peering through the darkness. The room looked empty. Empty, no furniture, nothing. I stepped on the cornice decorating the outer wall. The smell of mold hit my nose. I put one leg in, ready to climb over. Something grabbed my trousers and pulled me down.

Hanging halfway, one leg inside, the other one grabbed by something, most likely a dog's teeth, I gathered all my strength and moved my leg. Nothing. The more I kicked, the more it pulled. I relaxed my muscles until I felt the pulling weakened. Then I tensed them again, jerking my entire body and falling onto the floor of the room. I leaned out the window and saw half of a downspout bracket sticking from the wall. *Shit!* My nerves played a strange game with me. I closed the window and tiptoed to the door, images flashing in my mind of what could be behind it.

The door was locked. I pressed the handle a few more times. Nothing. Couldn't this be more complicated, please? Just opening the door, finding her, and running away wasn't enough.

I peered through the keyhole. There was a light on the other side. An ordinary lock. This would be easy. With help from a piece of wire I'd been carrying hidden in the sleeve of my jacket, I unlocked the door and left the door ajar. The passage was quiet. Crystal electric lamps hanging on the walls lit it.

A door opened. I heard fast-talking, and the door slammed. The series of sharp metallic clicks moved toward me. Someone in high heels. A woman in a green dress. I waited for the steps to disappear and sneaked out of the room. Scratching the spot right above the door handle with the wire, I marked it and closed it, making no noise.

Striding ahead, I tried to open the doors I passed. All doors were locked. Except the door at the end of the passage. I opened it and stepped into the room. The first thing that tickled my senses was the sweet scent of the perfume. Roses. Around twenty girls sat on the comfortable chairs or just stood around. A few of them held glasses of champagne. A few of them were drunk or had already been drugged. All of them stared at me. Doortje sat under the blinded window on the Victorian upholstered chair. Her gaze was way clearer than the last time I'd seen her.

I put my finger on my lips. "Shhh. I need to talk to her," I said, pointing at Doortje.

"You shouldn't be here," a girl beside me said in a low voice.

"None of you should be here. I'm her brother and want to talk to her." The good old reliable lie. I liked to be her brother.

Doortje said nothing.

"Brother?" said another one and put the empty champagne glass on the table behind her.

"Yes, brother."

"I wish my brother had come. I'd like to talk to him as well."

"Where's your brother?" another girl said.

"Dead."

"That's sad. I'm sorry to hear that," I said and moved further. "I believe you understand how important it is for me to talk to my sister."

They nodded.

Doortje gazed at us, still saying nothing.

"Doortje, our father is waiting. This is the last chance to be with him. Do you understand?"

She nodded and stood up.

"We have to hurry," I said, reaching with my hand.

She reached with her as well, but then hesitated.

The girls encouraged her.

"You don't need to be here."

"We won't tell you're gone."

"Go and say goodbye to your father."

"Go, Doortje. Go with your brother before the door opens," the girl said, and I spotted the white door right behind her.

"Father says sorry," I said.

Doortje, inspired by the unexpected support, stepped closer and took my hand.

"Good girl."

The white door opened, and we all stopped breathing. Wagner entered the room and stood there silently, gazing at us. After several seconds of silence, he spun and moved toward the still-open door.

Chapter 14

I released Doortje's hand and leaped forward like a tiger. Grabbing him by his shoulders, I tossed him back to the room and slammed the white door. Adrenaline took over. There was no room, no girls, no universe. Just him. And an intense urge to stop him.

I punched his neck from behind. It was weak and didn't knock him down. He spun, hauled off, and sprang his fist, aiming at my head. I blocked his blow and shot a hard, short punch direct to his nose.

Wagner jerked back, holding his face with both hands. He glanced at me. The blood flowed around his mouth. Running and bent, he hit my belly. We both fell to the floor, me under him, grasping each other's necks. I yanked him aside and rolled over. Something flew out of his jacket and slid across the floor, under the table and hit the wall. His Luger. Thank God it didn't shoot. Things were different now. Now, I sat on him.

I flung my fist, but he lifted his waist and twisted, throwing me aside. I fell over. Wagner jumped and pulled my shoulders back, leaping backward. His leg crossed the chair, and he fell on the floor. Like a rabbit, I hopped by him and bent, reaching forward. The girls grouped together, intimidated by the fight, hiding one behind the other. The nearest one grabbed the empty champagne bottle and smashed it right into my head.

"Oops. I'm sorry. I wanted to hit him, not you," she said, covering her mouth with her fingers.

Wagner chuckled and jumped to his feet. My eyes went foggy, and I was about to fall on the floor again. The room spun. Without knowing what I was doing and why, I ran forward, aiming to use the same trick he'd done before. I smashed my head into his abdomen and, lifting him a bit, I continued until my legs tangled. We fell onto the table, shattering glasses and bottles and making so much noise that even a deaf person would notice. His gorillas could come in anytime. I rolled away from him and sat on the floor. He sat, too. We stared at each other, panting like two rhinos, ready to charge again, but after a small nap.

The girls moved closer. Wagner sprang up, and before I could move, he grabbed Doortje by her hand and yanked her. The white door slammed again.

I grabbed his gun and checked it. It was fully loaded but not cocked.

"We need to go! All of you!" I said and opened the door I'd come in through.

"Why?" one girl said.

"He'll be back with his gorillas in no time."

"Why? Boys can't touch us. Wagner told them."

"He's pissed off. Let's hide," the blondie said. The others nodded.

They scurried but lingered.

"Take your high heels off!"

They obeyed. Way better. I found the mark on the door and opened it, letting the girls in.

"Wait here till I'm back! I will lock the door so no one can get in. And quiet, please. Don't open the window!"

"Where are you going? Don't leave us alone!" one girl said.

"Don't worry, I'll be back."

"No, you won't. I'm going with you."

I nudged her back. "I'm going to find Doortje, and then I will take you out of here. All of you."

"But tomorrow we are going on the trip. We can't leave."

Trip? So, it was true. That cynical jerk planned to get rid of them. Like tossing leftovers to dogs. I didn't want to scare them more than they were.

"Exactly! We are going on the trip, and I'm a bus driver."

"You said you were Doortje's brother."

"Brother and a bus driver. That's me," I said and closed the door, relocking it with the piece of wire.

Chapter 15

I ran along the passage, ripping the lamps off the wall. The darkness was my best friend tonight. Just finding Doortje and running away. I had eight bullets and no idea what was waiting for me.

The door in the room at the end of the passage was still open, and the light coming through it made a bright stripe in the darkness. I stuck to the light, and a bullet chipped the door frame ten inches from my head. I jerked back.

"Come over, mister detective, your sister's waiting!" Wagner's voice echoed from a distance.

"Let her go, Wagner!"

"Or what?"

The furniture rumbled. Someone was moving it. I took a few steps back, ran, and jumped through the stripe of the light. I spotted Wagner's gorilla with a submachine gun standing in the middle of the room. The white door was wide open. Behind it was the dance hall I knew from my first visit. Wagner stood there holding Doortje by her shoulders. Flying, I sent a bullet toward the big body without aiming. It hit the soft matter.

"You shot me!" a rough voice said.

The brief prelude of a submachine gun commenced, creating a set of holes in the walls. I knew that sound; the famous German MP40 or, as they said, *Maschinenpistole 40*. Three or four bullets flew close to my head. The walls were made of wood. A spit would pierce them.

"I hope you're dead, bastard!" His voice was weak.

The concert went on, involving more MP 40s and reaching the first crescendo.

I stretched out on the floor, hoping they wouldn't get the idea to aim down. Most of the bullets pierced through above my head. The noise tore at my ears. Then everything went silent. With one eye, I peered through the closest hole. Two other gorillas checked their colleague lying on the floor.

"He's dead!" one gorilla said.

They turned, their faces twisted in anger and changed the mags. I hurled myself onto the floor again. Two guns played the second act for me. Presto like from Vivaldi.

I couldn't be luckier, or it was the anger that controlled their brains. I didn't care. All bullets missed, cutting out a hole, big like an apple, in the wall. The shooting stopped when they emptied their magazines.

"Let him there and come over!" Wagner's voice resonated from the hall.

"We must bring him back, boss. That fucker got him!"

"Let him be where he is!"

"But boss, he deserves to be buried!"

Wagner shouted something I didn't pay attention to. It wasn't important. I peered through the hole. Both gorillas stood there, bending over their now-dead colleague. The man on the left straightened up. Two quick shots.

The bloke fell. The bullet punctured through his head. The second one got a metal greeting right to his buttock. He sprang and ran away, slamming the white door behind him. One wounded. Two down. Three shots. Not bad.

I moved in, Luger ready to bark. The first gorilla had a big blood stain on his chest. His shirt was wet from top to bottom. The shot had gone through his lungs. The second one lay in the pool of blood gushing from his head. I stuck the Luger behind the belt on my back, took his MP 40, and loaded it with the mag he had behind his belt. Another full mag came from the first gorilla. They wouldn't need them.

The engine of a truck roared outside. Voices, shouting, barking. One shot. A dog squealed.

I pulled the blind a bit. Soldiers scattered everywhere. Twenty, maybe thirty. Likely the fresh guards. Their commander headed toward the main entrance, accompanied by four gunners. One gorilla stopped him, talking about something. The commander must have asked some questions because the gorilla pointed at the house. The officer nodded, and one soldier shot the gorilla in the face. I jerked off the window, letting the blind fall back. Why would the guards have killed Wagner's bodyguard? What the hell was going on?

I looked around the room. I could pile the furniture and make a shelter. That would help for a short time. But I couldn't stand against overwhelming odds alone with two magazines only. I would empty them in less than one minute. I had five more bullets in Luger. That was like barking on the moon.

More shouting. More doors slammed. The submachine guns rattled.

Suddenly, the white door opened. I turned the table over and jumped behind it. Aiming the gun, I deadlocked, astonished.

Wagner entered the room, hiding behind Doortje and pushing her forward. He pressed another Luger against her neck.

"Now, mister detective, put the gun down and step aside!" he said, closing the door with his free hand and locking it.

"What are you doing, Wagner? Let her go! Leave her out of this!"

"Do as I say!"

Doortje's face was pale, her eyes wide. If anyone ever talked about terror, I would have her face in front of my eyes.

"Don't hide behind the girl, Wagner. Let's fight like men."

"Men? You're not a man. I'm really curious who the hell you are." His eyes threw lightning toward me.

He continued. "Now, do as I say. Put the gun down and step aside."

"No."

He pushed the gun more until Doortje screamed. His dirty hand covered her mouth.

"All right, all right," I said and put the MP 40 on the floor.

He chuckled and aimed his Luger at me. The muffled voices of soldiers reverberated from behind the white door. In an instant, they would reach the hall.

"Say goodbye, bastard!"

Wagner pulled the trigger. I threw myself down. The shot chipped the table two inches from where I'd had my head. I drew the pistol from behind my belt and rolled, sending two bullets at him. The first one shattered the window, but the second scratched his shoulder right when he shot again. His bullet hit the ceiling.

Someone shouted, and the door shook violently.

"*Scheize!*" Wagner said and tossed Doortje away. She fell. He ran toward the passage and disappeared.

Doortje was scared but not injured. She could stand up. I took her by the hand, and we ran down the dark passage as well. No traces of Wagner. Touching the wall, I found and unlocked the door, and we slipped in, closing it behind us. The girls screamed. I heard the white door crack.

"Shhh!" I said, fighting with the lock. My hands trembled. The deadbolt got stuck. Adrenaline rushed through my veins in a fresh wave. Voices were getting louder. The soldiers must have reached the passage. I wiped the sweat off my forehead and tried again. The soldiers rattled the other locked doors. I saw a beam of a flashlight through the keyhole. The steps were approaching. A rumble and a blast of splintering wood. Perhaps I could hold the door against the soldiers. I pressed against it. The door moved a hundredth of an inch. The wire spun, and the lock clicked.

The door handle fluttered. We didn't breathe. The handle moved again. Someone swore in German.

"*Wir haben ihn gefunden!* We found him!" a muffled voice came through the closed window.

"*Was?!* What?!" a voice shouted from behind the door.

"*Sie haben ihn gefunden.* They found him," said another voice from behind the door.

The steps of heavy boots echoed away. Exhale.

This would be too much even for an elephant. The adrenaline rush wobbled, and the old pain took over me again. Everything hurt. It was so intense I almost fainted. My knees bent. The girls surrounded me and helped me back on my feet.

Someone yelled outside. We turned toward the window, keeping our distance.

The Nazi officer had a bunch of flyers in his hand and waved them before Wagner's face. The man kneeled, held by two soldiers. His shoulder was bleeding. Three gorillas next to him on their knees as well. He stared right at the window we stood behind. He couldn't see us; the darkness of the room shielded us.

The Nazi officer pulled the gun, cocked it, and shot one gorilla in the face. Then another one. The last gorilla fidgeted but got his portion, too. The girls pressed their clenched fists against their mouths and didn't breathe. Wagner still stared at the window. An invisible force pulled my eyes as if he locked them. The officer aimed the gun at him. Wager grinned. The finger moved. Wagner jerked his head and fell back cold.

Chapter 16

The coffee was excellent. I nodded at Carl, waving the cup. He poured me another one.

"Did you enjoy breakfast?"

"Yes, Carl. Perfect as always," I said.

"You should go and sleep till morning. You look like you passed through the stone mill. Being a woman, I would run away from you."

I grinned. "Thank God, you're not a woman."

I sat at the counter at Carl's diner. The sun was grinning at me through the windows. Everything that had happened two days ago was a hazy memory. I'd been drinking a lot for the last forty-eight hours to get rid of that experience.

Carl returned from the kitchen and whispered, "Just got information that the old man and his daughter are all right. I thought it would be interesting for you to know."

I nodded. "Thanks, Carl."

Carl laughed. "And what now, Mr. Private Eye?"

"I don't know. Do you have another case for me?"

"No, unless you'd like to figure out who stole my old bicycle."

"You had no bicycle, Carl."

"The case is solved," Carl said and chuckled.

"You owe me a hundred bucks."

He nodded and poured another cup of coffee. "This is on me. I appreciate you giving the money to the Achters family. Bram's mother deserved better treatment."

"Don't mention it. The old man gave me more than I needed. If someone found it in my flat, it would be a one-way ticket, you know where."

Carl blew me a kiss.

"You're a hero, Erik."

"No, I'm not. I kept a huge portion for myself."

"That's all right. You eat the bread as well. And you buy it from me. That's better."

Someone touched my arm. I turned. A teenage boy stood behind me, and handed me a folded paper. I took it, and he left without saying a word.

I opened the paper. "*Meet you at Ernest. 19:00 sharp. Anna Bakker.*"

"What is that?" Carl said.

I showed him, and he whistled.

"Do you know her?" I said.

"Who do you think got the old man and his daughter out of the country? And the other girls?"

I waved the paper, and Carl nodded.

"That's it, my boy. She's a good mentor for blokes like you. I bet she has the case you asked for. And I'm telling you, it smells like big money."

Carl took the paper from my hands and burned it in an ashtray.

"That lady plays a high game. No one knows whom she works for. Maybe the resistance. Maybe Dutch government-in-exile."

"Should I be afraid?"

"You know what? Just go there. I'm sure you won't regret it. More coffee?"

ABOUT THE AUTHOR

After working for decades as a software developer, Jack Tenor finally retired. The power of storytelling had always captivated him, and now that he had more free time, he felt compelled to try his hand at writing his own stories. The click-clack of the keyboard is reminiscent of his days of coding complex algorithms. But this time, instead of lines of code, he was weaving together sentences and paragraphs to create vivid narratives.

Printed in Great Britain
by Amazon